STONECUTTER

JON J MUTH
JOHN KURAMOTO

FEIWEL AND FRIENDS
NEW YORK

A FEIWEL AND FRIENDS BOOK
An Imprint of Macmillan

STONECUTTER. Text copyright © 1994 by John Kuramoto.
Illustrations copyright © 1994, 2009 by Jon J Muth. All rights reserved.
Printed in China. For information, address Feiwel and Friends, 175 Fifth Avenue,
New York, N.Y. 10010.

Library of Congress Cataloging-in-Publication Data

Muth, Jon J.
Stonecutter / Jon J Muth ; written by John Kuramoto.
— 1st Feiwel and Friends ed.   p. cm.
Summary: A stonecutter wants to be everything he is not and has to
learn the hard way that what he really wants to be is exactly who he is.
ISBN-13: 978-0-312-55456-9 / ISBN-10: 0-312-55456-7
[1. Folklore—Japan.] I. Kuramoto, John. II. Title.
PZ8.1.M966Sto 2009 398.2—dc22 [E] 2008034744

Book design by Barbara Grzeslo
Feiwel and Friends logo designed by Filomena Tuosto

Originally published in the United States by Donald M. Grant
First Feiwel and Friends Edition: April 2009

10 9 8 7 6 5 4 3 2 1

www.feiwelandfriends.com

or my
boys, my life
treasures

Allen & Marcus

the World is yours
I love you ♥Mom

Christmas 2010

STONECUTTER

The stonecutter stood before the stone,
deciding where to begin.

When at last he chose the proper spot,
he drove the chisel into the stone with the
hammer.

The work was long, and slow, and difficult.

The stonecutter's hands were as
strong and rough as the stone they cut.

As he worked, the stonecutter thought to himself, "This stone is as old as the earth, and will be here long after I am gone."

"Each night I go home covered in dust millions of years old."

"Each morning I go to cut stones again,
just as I have done my entire life.

Is there nothing more for me?"

The stonecutter chiseled the stone into blocks, cutting each block according to the stone's natural shape.

"Perhaps this will be made into bricks for a temple, or a wealthy man's palace."

"Perhaps it will be carved into a beautiful sculpture."

"But I have only uncarved blocks to offer."

The stone yielded to the stonecutter's tools in fragments, taking shape under his hands.

"I have no authority. I have no power."

When he finished the stone block, he took it to town to sell.

There he passed by many merchants,
and finally sold his block to one of them.

The stonecutter looked at the merchant,
wearing clothes rich and fine.

And he knew that the merchant would sell the stone block for much more money than he had given the stonecutter, without the slightest labor on his part.

The stonecutter cursed his aching back.

He cursed his poverty and lowly status.

.

He cursed the past that brought him here
and the future that would take him nowhere.

He decided to abandon his life as a stonecutter and become a merchant.

And so he became a merchant,
trading things instead of making them,
and he became very rich.

He lived in luxury,

without having to work hard,

for now there were others to do the hard work

for him.

His hands became delicate and soft, his manners refined.

Other people envied his good fortune.

But one day, a high official passed by
in a grand procession, and everyone,
rich or poor, had to bow down to him.

And the merchant realized that although he had become very rich trading things, he had no influence over people.

"There is real power," he thought,
and abandoned his life as a merchant
to become a high official.

And so he became a high official,
carried everywhere he went, feared and cursed
by those who knelt before him.

He no longer had to barter and haggle;
the high official gave orders,
and his subjects obeyed.

His proclamations affected many people,
though he saw very few.

As he sat in his elegant chair,

the sun beat down upon him in his robes,

and he became very hot and uncomfortable.

His servants fanned him, but it did little good.

As a high official, he could not leave his chair, nor remove his robes.

He realized that for all his power over people,

he needed people to be powerful.

"How magnificent is the sun," he thought,
and abandoned his life as a high official
to become the sun.

And so he became the sun, high above the earth, lighting the sky.

The sun would be in his place day after day,
without fail.

No one dared look at him.

If he felt like it, he could make their days warm
and pleasant, or he could make them hot
and unbearable.

The sun began each morning
in the same place at one end of the sky,
and ended each evening at the same place
at the other end of the sky.

Despite his brightness, the sun could only be in his prescribed place.

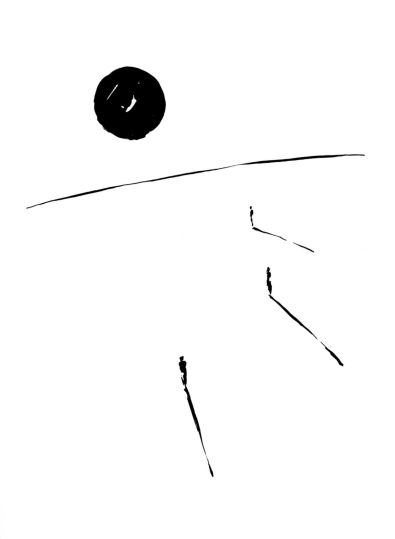

One day, a cloud passed in front of him, darkening his rays, and he saw that the cloud could change shape, and even block him, the sun.

And so he became the cloud,
darkening the skies.

He grew larger and larger,
encompassing the skies.

He made himself all manner of shapes,
and he found that he could make rain.
The rain was welcomed by some
and cursed by others.

The cloud could shower upon them
and rejuvenate,
or flood them and destroy.

But, though he could block the sun
and drench the land,
he could not touch either.

Then a wind came, blowing him from the sky,
and the cloud saw that for all his power over the
sun and the earth,
he could only come between them.

And so he became the wind,

constantly changing, unseen but felt by all.

He brought in clouds or blew them away.

He dried the sweat of workers or kept them from working.

He blew the leaves from trees and roofs from houses.

There seemed to be nothing the wind could not move, no force more powerful than he.

He was all shapes, and all sizes,
and all strengths.

He could be anywhere, and touch anything.

But he came upon a huge stone,

and though he mustered all his power,

he could not move the stone.

For all his power, the stone remained undisturbed.

When the wind realized that the stone
could not be influenced, he saw in it
an absolute, undeniable power.

And so he became the stone,
stronger than any force,
as old as time.

Though he could not move,
neither could he be moved.

The stone confronted any weather,
and did not change his shape.

He was strength itself,
more powerful than anything else on earth
or in the sky.

The stonecutter stood before the stone,

deciding where to begin.

THANK YOU TO JEAN FEIWEL FOR HER TERRIFIC
AND CONSISTENT VISION. THANK YOU TO ALLEN SPIEGEL
FOR MAKING THIS BOOK HAPPEN, TWICE.
THANK YOU TO BALLARD, TERRY, ZHANG HONG NIAN,
AND ROBERT STORM FOR ALL THEIR WORK.
THANK YOU TO BONNIE, FOR ALWAYS.
AND GREAT THANKS TO LIZ SZABLA
FOR BEING THIS BOOK'S GENEROUS
AND INSIGHTFUL SHEPHERD.

—JON J MUTH, 2008